Praise for
The Bachelor's Cat

"A must have for the cat lover."

"Funny and smart and endearing, with language that flows as smoothly as the fairy tale it evokes. . . . A story that connects emotionally, and should be on everyone's 'to read' list."

"James Stewart in *It's a Wonderful Cat*."

THE
BACHELOR'S
CAT

A Love Story

L. F. HOFFMAN

HarperPaperbacks
A Division of HarperCollinsPublishers

🔥 HarperPaperbacks
A Division of HarperCollins*Publishers*
10 East 53rd Street, New York, NY 10022-5299

This is a work of fiction. The characters, incidents, and
dialogues are products of the author's imagination and are
not to be construed as real. Any resemblance to actual
events or persons, living or dead, is entirely coincidental.

ISBN 0-06-109813-2

HarperCollins®, 🔥®, and HarperPaperbacks™ are
trademarks of HarperCollins Publishers Inc.

Cover illustration © 1999 by Elizabeth Harbour

A hardcover edition of this book was published in 1997
by HarperCollins*Publishers*.

First HarperPaperbacks printing: February 1999

Printed in the United States of America

Visit HarperPaperbacks on the World Wide Web at
http://www.harpercollins.com

❖ 10 9 8 7 6 5 4 3 2 1

To A Fine Romance
by Dr. Judith Sills,
the book that explains it all,
and
to Spike, my own personal
bachelor's cat

*O*nce upon a time there was a bachelor, a romantic and difficult man. This is the story of how the bachelor found a stray cat and how that cat helped the bachelor find love.

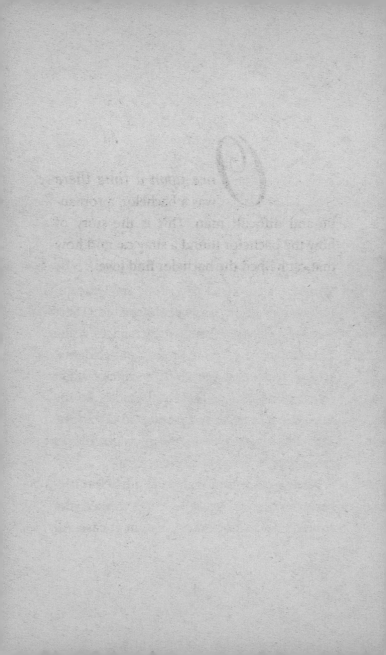

The opening of his exhibit attracted a hundred people or so. Unfortunately, they were the wrong hundred. There were a few friends, some acquaintances, some boredom victims, and dozens of accidental scurriers through the coldest January night that had hit Philadelphia in decades. By the time the temperature dropped to six above, the exhibit was the warmest place for blocks around.

The bachelor, in jeans and a black turtleneck with a white silk scarf, worked the room. He was not exactly a man at ease. All of his small supply of cash and most of his even smaller stock of credit had been spent on the printing, the framing, the invitations, the poster.

His work looked like he did, like a thing built up from contradictory layers, slick graphics barely concealing an ironic sensibility. A luscious seated nude framed with lit propane torches stared matter-of-factly at the viewer. A dozen orange Halloween masks blew across a black beach framed by waterfalls. It was work that was meant by its very nature to be misunderstood, and to no one's surprise but the artist's, it was.

The bachelor had moved to Philadelphia some nine months before in a spring that seemed full of promise. This exhibit was the key to his marketing plan and it was going horribly wrong—it had gone wrong from the beginning. The expensively printed poster showing a full-length nude of a somewhat distracted woman supporting a window-sash picture frame that enclosed a gigantic doll's arm had been denied space in shop windows all over town. He was surprised, even a little hurt.

The pitches to individual galleries and ad agencies had been politely received. There had even been some encouraging moments. But the crowd in the gallery was still made up mostly of people who were just glad to be indoors and drinking. Compliments were not being converted into sales and the crowd was thinning. His girlfriend, impatient with his attentions to everyone but her, left with another man.

The next morning he woke up cold in his small rowhouse. He had turned down the heat to conserve his supply of oil. He put a bathrobe over the clothes he had slept in and went downstairs. He wrapped the coffee grinder in a towel to shield his hangover from the noise and pulverized some of the dark French roast beans. He took two aspirins and a vitamin C and felt the cold again, this time from the inside out.

As he drank the coffee there was time to pick at the scab of what he was doing in this town, this house, in his barely moving career. There was time to think about his girlfriend, but not the energy to be angry. The windows rattled in the wind, and he heard the rattles as accusations. He stood still with his coffee cup pointing south in front of him, and his heart spun from recrimination to regret to sadness to shame.

Then he heard someone else crying—a baby? The sound was coming from right outside his front door. You might think that he was too percolated through with self-pity to investigate, but you'd be wrong. There was a species of people a long time ago that didn't respond automatically to a baby's cry, and they are, naturally enough, extinct. The artist was, in several important respects, dead, but his kind was not extinct.

Through the open door he felt a face full of cold, then the heat of the cup on his knuckles and the warmth of the coffee steam's cloud reaching his chin. The crying was coming from a gray kitten, tinier than most kittens that he'd seen. It had tucked itself into the lee of his stoop, its ears plastered to its head.

It saw him, or maybe it got a scent of the slightly warmer air from the open door. Here was a creature that filled an unthinkable slot in the universe: She was visibly more miserable than he was. She looked more uncomfortable than he did and, if cats can be allowed, had more reason for despair.

He saw some men across the street, horsing a few pieces of furniture into a house. Moving day, he thought, and somebody lost their kitten: Down the stoop, pick up kitten, shout across. Wind cuts through the bathrobe. Negative, negatory, uh-uh. Ain't our cat, pal—and don't you try to palm it off on us either.

He picked up the cat and carried it to the

top of the steps. In his hand he could see how infantile she was—barely a cat, more like an embryo, almost womb-wet, some unspecific baby four-footer. He put her down on the top step, his hand pulling back quickly from the little suggestion of fertility she brought with her. Later, he would remember noticing the subtle light and dark stripes along her back.

He was slipping into a Flotsam Phase, feeling feckless, carrying a bad case of shrunken heart. He couldn't just bring a cat into the house. Okay, maybe he could, if she wanted to come.

She looked up at him as he pushed the door open. He actually said, "Do you want to come in?" It didn't seem anywhere near as silly at the time as it does now. She ran inside and he followed her, closing out the cold behind them.

From the middle of the living-room

floor she cried. He picked her up again, for a moment more impressed with her size than with her need. Tail and all, she just covered the palm of his hand. This was a cat that had been taken from her mother. He recalled an image from an early-morning kids' TV show: a baby bird being fed from an eyedropper.

He had milk. He put some on her nose, some on a spoon, and then more in a saucer. He knew she needed more than this, and he knew that he had no money in the house. Nothing. Another regret, but he felt this one more sharply than the others—a hot stab, not a cold, dead ache.

Pockets and bureau drawers and the crack in the sofa yielded one dollar and seventy-seven cents. He dressed with a purpose and went to the corner deli. There was a sign: "Liverwurst on sale—$1.77 for a half pound." The stupidity of coincidence would ordinarily have made him laugh. Today it made him ask for exactly half a pound.

When he opened the door of the house, she was standing, crying. Looking at him and the open door, she fled. He found her under the couch, crying again. He lured her out slowly with kissing sounds and the smell of his package.

He made a paste from the liverwurst and milk and fed it to her on the flat end of a toothpick. He trimmed her little needle claws with his nail clipper and she didn't struggle. A few minutes later, she was asleep and he took her upstairs, laid her on his bed, and put a soft sweater over her.

What to do with a kitten? He obviously couldn't have a cat. Obviously. Wasn't home much or something like that; what if he had to go to Istanbul or got a portrait assignment in Florence? Besides, this was somebody else's kitten—a strayed creature, not a free one. It was a straightforward ethical matter.

He called the doorstop local newspaper, the one that showed up on his stoop every Friday. It took ads for lost pets, no charge. His ad read:

FOUND

SMALL GRAY FEMALE KITTEN.
TO CLAIM OR ADOPT HER,
CALL 555-0588

The ad wouldn't appear for a few days. While he waited, he learned that the kitten ate ten or twelve times a day, calling when she was hungry. As she got stronger, she would find him and cry for food.

The kitten slept that first night tucked into his armpit. He was an emotional man but not sentimental. He knew she was snuggling up to his body heat and not to him, but at the moment a little exchange seemed like a good idea.

The kitten screamed once in the night and he brought her food, relieved that it was hunger and not terror that he had to deal with.

He woke up warmer the next morning, and he even smiled at the two tiny turds he found in the bathroom next to the toilet. He cut down a cardboard box, filled it with shredded newspapers, and put her in it. The kitten brushed at the papers with her paw, pushing some behind her and some to the side. When she tried to get out of the box and couldn't scale the walls, he cut her a doorway in the box and folded the flap down to make a ramp. He smiled again and pronounced himself a litter-box architect, a field he might consider taking up.

*His next days were occu-*pied with trying to salvage something from the wreckage of his exhibit. A few clients were personally invited, a gallery owner came to visit. He turned up a few pieces of respectable freelance work and knocked out a portrait. He ransomed his dry cleaning, bought cat food and heating oil.

When his home-built litter box, which he had christened Falling Water, started to stink, he replaced it with a proper plastic one. He didn't cut a gateway in it, figuring that he would use the tray for some other purpose after the kitten's owner reclaimed her. She had grown enough to throw herself over the edges anyway.

That night he was sitting in an armchair stroking her. She sat between his legs with her front feet on top of his left thigh. He ran the back of his index finger between her ears, down her back, and along her tail. She squeezed her eyes with pleasure as his nail passed her neck. She made a tiny rumbling sound from her throat. It startled him at first and then he found himself strumming this sound out of her. He wondered if there were any jobs in the Philadelphia Orchestra playing first kitten.

Every few strokes she dug her claws into

the thick denim of his pant leg and he would stop stroking, squeeze her paws, and say "no." And so they fell into a rhythm: stroke, stroke, stroke, dig, squeeze pinch, "no," stroke, stroke. The intervals between the "no's" got longer, and the bachelor lost himself for a while.

Then he very slowly formed the thought that this might be a forever moment, a little suspension of time and thought. But then he remembered that moments like these always get interrupted and that made him self-conscious, which made him lose the moment. So in the flash of a brain wave, being happy had made him sad and the stroking suddenly seemed as if he were doing it with someone else's hand.

But he kept on running his finger down her back and she kept on purring, and somehow she teased him back into the present. Then the phone rang.

He had reasons for wanting to answer the phone, but he didn't want to leave this cat. So he picked her up, unpeeled her surprised claws from his leg, and placed her on his shoulder. Together they went to the phone.

She cried a little and held on to his shirt. He steadied her with his hand, petted her, and barely managed to attend to his phone call. For the rest of the night, he transported her by shoulder. She got the hang of it, balancing with only the slightest amount of claw grip.

There was another call a few minutes later from the girlfriend last seen on exhibit night. She didn't apologize for leaving him and barely mentioned the other man. The purpose of her call, he guessed, was to dangle herself in front of him, to see if he'd bite. He was angry, he bit, he yelled; she yelled back. It was his fault, her fault, and they hung up exhausted with each other.

The next day the ad came
out. He picked up the newspaper from his stoop and found the lost pet listing. He congratulated himself. Good citizen. He hoped the cat's owner was reading the ad, too. It would be nice, he thought, if she went back to her family. They probably missed her.

He spent the morning working on stock photography, and in the afternoon he visited a city agency that hired some freelance artists. Coming home, he heard the kitten scrambling, rushing, throwing herself away from the opening door and hiding under the couch.

The kitten had grown. She was now as big as most kittens are when they leave their mothers. She had come into her species. She carried, without boasting, a full kitten face: big ears, startling yellow-gold eyes, disproportionate whiskers.

She sat on his lap that night while he read. She made that miraculous little sound again. He was goofy enough to think that it was something personal, a private gift from her to him. There was no one around to remind him that the sound was just purring and that all cats purr.

The phone rang around nine P.M. It was a

woman's voice, middle-aged and kindly.

"I saw your ad in the *Girard Home News* and I was wondering if that kitten was still up for adoption?"

He was shocked; a jolt ran down his middle from his throat to his seat. For a second he felt actual rage at this inoffensive soul on the other end of the line. Was she going to come and rip this kitten—his kitten—away from his bosom? His kitten, yes. Of course, how obvious, how weird. His kitten, her person.

He caught himself in time. "No, thank you, ma'am. She's already found a home."

A few days later, a friend who had been following the kitten story from a distance asked him if he was really going to keep her. "Yes," he replied, thinking of the girlfriend and the girlfriend before that. "I want to see if I can actually have a long-term relationship that I don't screw up." This kitten had stirred something in him.

His enthusiasm for work gradually came back. A few small successes, a check, then two. The girlfriend was back, too. She was not much impressed by the kitten, but the girlfriend also stirred something in him.

She remarked that it was a very ordinary little cat and told her friends that he had "taken in an alley cat." She made fun of him when he left her bed early in the morning to go home to feed the kitten. He tried to get the girlfriend in on the fun, seduce her into sharing this little cuteness with him. Hearing another creature referred to as "cute" was not her idea of fun, however. She told him that she thought it interesting that he "found another female" the very next day after their last breakup.

In spite of her bad cat attitude, the return of the girlfriend made him happy. It made him more troubled, too. He had taken to thinking of her as his Mixed Blessing—he even introduced her that way once. Her face was exotic, Europe and Asia in it, high cheekbones and ferocious eyes. Her body was small and hyperfeminine, and she had tended it well: smooth curves and hard muscles. She was an understanding and sensitive woman, but no longer a gentle one. Time and disappointment had made her a mercenary. It was as if she had taken her skills at navigating the human soul and signed aboard a pirate ship with them.

He was still a romantic, which was, he realized later, a recipe for more disappointment. They had their own amorous cycle. For a week or two, or maybe a month, they would come together, passionate and close. Then she would find someone who could soothe her fears. Someone who was not young, creative, and broke. So she would follow her fears and hurt his heart, but the older, richer guy never really wanted her for more than a while, so she and the bachelor would come back together with tears and kisses. He had learned the cycle and came to rely on her infidelity as his own escape from closeness. He soothed the time in between the girlfriend with other women.

The bachelor and the kit-

ten were sitting in their armchair. He was reading; she was protesting his reading by pushing at his book-holding hand with her nose. The doorbell rang; he stuffed his book in the cushion crack and walked to the door. The kitten jumped to the arm of the chair and watched him. He looked back over his shoulder at her, mostly in the spirit of continuing their battle over whether books are for reading or for scratching.

She was not watching him with her usual playful fascination. There was an agitation in her tiny head jerks that worked its way down through her body in spastic waves. She was scared; he was puzzled. As he opened the door for the paperboy, she fled, adrenaline-mad, for the safety of a spot beneath the couch.

A few minutes later, he was lying on the floor trying to distinguish the cat from the dust bunnies in her hiding spot. "Come on out, honey. It was just the paperboy . . . other people's pimples can't hurt you. . . ." And then he made the connection: Of course, it was her fear of being outside, cold and crying.

He knew a thing or two about being frightened. He would help her get over it. The first step, he decided, was to give her a name. How could you have self-confidence if you didn't even have a self to be confident in? It had to be a tough name: no Fluffy or Max or Annabelle. Something feminine but not frilly: Tiger was okay but not very personal, and Duke lacked a sense of humor. Frankie. Yes, Frankie—strong, steady, a pal you can count on. Good for a laugh, good for a hug. Good ol' Frankie.

Out from under the couch and in his arms, she felt him petting her as he whispered, "Frankie . . . Frankie . . . Frankie . . ." He chanted her new name as he was getting her food ready and she twitched her tail to the beat of his saying it.

In the bedroom, once he was sure she had followed him, he balled up a sock and waved it at her, saying her name again. She leaped to him.

In a week or so, "Frankie" had become the sound that meant food and petting and fun. So, of course, whenever she heard it, she came to check out whatever good stuff awaited her.

His friends were all amazed. They had

never heard of a cat coming when she was called. He accepted compliments on her behalf. He refused to completely deny suggestions that "he had a way with animals." He laughed a lot to himself.

In the meantime, the kit-
ten was domesticating him. He had been
proud of a very efficient way he had with
the household trash. Grocery bags—paper
inside plastic—stood upright in his kitchen
next to his home-built countertop. Scraps
and wrappings went directly into the bag
until it was filled and the plastic handles
tied.

The filled bags were lined up on the back
porch until garbage day, when they were
stacked neatly at the curb. The bachelor
liked the eco-sense of it. No extra trash gen-

erated to take care of the trash.

The kitten liked the arrangement, too. There was always a wonderfully smelly toy to beat and bat and claw through. And then there was great stuff to eat and more things to play with. She didn't even mind the coffee grounds that spilled on the floor and stuck to her paws.

It took the bachelor a week or so to admit that he had to buy a trash can— something big and ugly and plastic. So, muttering to himself about fossil fuels and signing up for the Bourgeois Brigade, he lugged home a thirty-gallon monster with lid.

He was proud of their growing friendship, although the cat still ran from the clicking sound of his key in the door. She had picked a few different spots to hide, seeking the nearest shelter when she heard the dreaded Click of Doom. She was easier to tease out now, but he felt bad for her, knew all about the fear of being left out in the cold. He wished that she would learn to trust that his homecoming meant something warm.

There was a day, after the spring equinox and before April Fool's Day, when he thought they had made a breakthrough. The day was warm and windy. The contrast between the stuffiness of his house and the fresh, wet earth smell of outside drove him to domestic action. He put the cat on her perch on his shoulder and went to the top floor of his three-story rowhouse. He opened all the windows on the third floor and felt the rush of stale air chimneying its way out.

He spoke softly to her, saying her name

and stopping after each window-opening to pet her. She clung to him as he bent and lifted, curious but unafraid. On the second floor, she jumped off for a minute and batted a sock ball. He put her back on his shoulder and continued opening windows.

By the first floor, he was feeling pretty smug. They had conquered this fear of hers—all it took was the right approach. He was beginning to think that maybe he did have a special way with animals.

When he opened the large window that looked out on the street, the spell broke. She hissed, a fleck of cat spit hit the window frame. She dug her claws into his shoulder, head-faked a move to the left, and pushed herself off hard to the right. She hit the ground with too much momentum, skidded on her face across the hardwood floor, recovered, and made for the couch. It was an hour before she came out.

His times with the girl-
friend were hot, incandescent, fusion temperature. It was all different now, and he wanted to live his life in the fiery spinning of this love. This was the fourth or fifth reprise of their relationship. He thought he would have become used to it by now. Each time they got back together, he felt more intensely; each time they broke up, he was more devastated than the time before. That night, he found himself petting the cat and wishing it were this simple with the girl-friend. Why, he wondered, couldn't it be

simple purring pleasure instead of white-hot, burn-yourself-with-yourself heat? Then he found himself wondering if thoughts like this were the reason that romantic comedies got a bad name.

Another spring day, when the cherry blossoms had already fallen and some serious rebirth was under way, the bachelor took a weekday trip to the mountains for some trout fishing with two of his buddies.

They left in the dark and when the sun came up, they annoyed the trout for a while. By ten o'clock they were eating red pepper sandwiches with shavings of provolone and genoa salami, and congratulating themselves on being smart enough to have jobs that they could leave for a day. The bachelor thought once or twice about how he and the girlfriend might have enjoyed the stream.

Coming home, he caught the cat napping, heard the scratching sounds of her claws on the wood floor as she ran for her hiding spot. He tapped the end of his fishing rod on the floor in front of the couch. Slow time.

Tap.

Tap . . . taptap . . . taptaptap.

A paw from the shadow of a cave: tentative, taptap, swat.

TAPTAPTAP. Retreat.

Tap a few inches farther out: taptap.

Lunge—bared claws seize it.

Freeze.

The bachelor was laughing, and the kitten, who had been invested in the seriousness of the moment, was brought up short from her prey. She looked at him and then away, paused for a moment, and stalked away.

The bachelor had an idea. Within a minute or two, he returned with his fishing rod rerigged. He had removed the reel and tied one end of a piece of fuzzy brown twine around the reel seat. Then he threaded the rest of the twine through the guides and out the tip of the rod. He left about eight feet of line dangling. Next he made a lure, winding another eight feet of twine into a coil around his thumb and little finger. He cinched the coil in the center with a few turns of twine, making a figure eight. Then he cut a few of the loops just at the point where they entered the binding. The cut ends dangled, fuzzy and inviting. He tied the lure to the end of the line and he was ready.

Sneaking up on her in stocking feet, he pulled some line away from the rod with his left hand. That brought the lure closer up to the rod tip. He waited until she was looking away. With a flip, he tossed the lure over and just beyond her. She jumped back and then forward in the space of a blink. She threw herself at the lure only to see it jump straight up and away from her claws as she skidded clumsily along the floor. He had pulled some line away from the rod without moving the rod itself. She looked up, calculating distances, estimating escape velocities.

The lure descended; she leaped, twisting in the air, missing, and landing uncatlike, with a tiny thud on the wooden floor. Then the lure skittered away and she ran after it, misjudging the traction of the floor only once or twice.

He knew from the shadows that he spent a long time playing, although it seemed as if no time at all had passed. It reminded him of the timelessness he used to feel in a trout stream.

It was getting time for the girlfriend to leave again. Summer was coming and there were men with exciting places at the shore, maybe even trips to Europe. He wondered if she would manufacture a fight or just announce that she needed "a little space to experience all of who I am."

Sometimes he thought that she had a thermostat inside, that when his love for her grew hot enough, it tripped the switch and broke their circuit. Other times, he knew that he really had nothing to do with it.

So when she broke a date for a weekend trip to the country, he was not surprised. She told him on the Thursday before they were to leave that she was "going exploring" with her girlfriend instead. Somehow, their date "just didn't feel right anymore." Their guaranteed room reservations? Well, if he wasn't going to be using them, maybe she and her friend could. Probably wouldn't be able to pay him for a while. . . . Sorry, but he did understand the importance of going with your feelings, didn't he? He almost admired her craftsmanship, but mostly, over the next few weeks, he felt sad and a little ashamed of himself.

He cried from time to time, more often than you might think, almost always holding the cat. Sometimes he would seek her out when the sadness of it all got to him; sometimes she would hear him and come. He realized, of course, that she knew his

tears were the signal of a time to be stroked
and hugged, but he let himself think she
knew more than that.

The worst thing of all was that he couldn't
even pretend anymore that he loved the girlfriend, although he told her that he did and
even thought it on the outside layer of his
soul. Alone at night, he knew that he had
come to need her to enjoy any feeling of life
and that need, not love, was the gravity that
kept him in her orbit.

Spring passed, then sum-
mer. He worked enough to pay his bills and
passed the time with friends and projects.
He dated a few women whom he met at his
neighborhood bar and worked on a new
set of pictures for another exhibit. From
time to time he would run into women
friends of the girlfriend. Some of them
would offer the kind of quick sympathy
that's usually reserved for the harmlessly
pathetic. Others would be more kindly and
sometimes he dated them, too. The cat still
jumped onto his bed at night, although she

waited until the bed was quiet.

On nights when he slept alone she would climb up on his chest and adopt the sphinx posture just at the edge of the covers. He would wake up in the morning to find her staring at him, their noses inches apart. Occasionally he would sing, in his best Rex Harrison talking-blues voice, "Why can't a woman be more like a cat?" He guessed that there was a relationship between his experiences with each of these females and that it wasn't a trivial one. He knew that there was some point to grasp, but he shrank from it. He was barely able to make out that the cat liked him and the girlfriend didn't. But that was as far as he got.

He was by now an offi-
cial cat owner. He even began to answer to
the name "cat person." He learned that people were willing to ascribe their dumbest cat
stereotypes directly to the cat owner.

It went like this: A person would hear
that he had a cat and offer with wrinkled
nose, "Cats are so standoffish." Sometimes a
soul who had read an entire psychology
book would leap to "You must be a very
reserved person."

In his novice cat-owning period, he
would argue. He would even find himself

telling adorable stories about the cat. Fortunately, he caught himself before he became an official bore. By the time he took his final cat vows, he had retreated to smiling silence on the matter. To his surprise, as soon as he gave up defending the cat, his friends jumped in and did it for him. He knew there was a lesson in this, too, somewhere, but he was content to leave it unlearned.

His clubhouse that sum-
mer was a neighborhood bar. It was the best
possible bar: It had an interior that had just
become old and a crowd that was still plau-
sibly young. He dropped in almost every
night. People left messages for him there
and sometimes people left there with him.
Except for nights when the girlfriend would
cross town to show up surrounded by
admirers, it was a pretty comfortable place.

On Wednesday nights, a funky blues
band played there. The bachelor showed up
one Wednesday just as a young acquain-

tance of his arrived. The boy was carrying a flute case, hoping to sit in for a set, wishing perhaps to keep the long tradition of blues flute music alive in yet another venue. They went in together, found the band setting up, and saw a knot of women in the middle of the bar. They were laughing, hanging out together. They had the look of women who had forgotten about men for the night and wanted to enjoy one another.

Nonetheless, probabilities being what probabilities are, the bachelor and the blues flautist took up stations near them, positioning themselves at the bar with a few introductory, smiling "Excuse mes."

The women remained facing inward, held in place by some gravity of their own. The bachelor and his friend ordered drinks. In the bar mirror, the bachelor could see a few appraising glances, an elbow or two, a dipped head, a pointing chin. Signs of

potential comet activity, he thought—someone ready to break free and go spinning
through space.

In a minute or two, as amplifiers were
adjusted and guitars tuned, they felt a pres-
sure wave of shifting postures at the bar. A
woman had popped up alongside the
flautist. She was chubby-cheeked and smiling, with green eyes and honey-brown hair.
She nodded to him, started a conversation
with the boy, and the bachelor smiled.
Grown-up woman was about to teach a little boy a thing or two. This woman was
much closer to his age than she was to the
kid's.

The bachelor listened to them for a
while. In a few sentences, the woman's per-
sonality started to emerge. She was perky
without being vacant, humorous but wise-
eyed. Not quite right for the lad with the
flute. The bachelor figured he'd watch for a

while, introduce himself, and see if he could pull one of the woman's thinner friends into the conversation.

The woman, he overheard, was a native Philadelphian. She had been living in Los Angeles for a few years and just moved back. The boy asked her how she liked California and she said something about all the houses having exercise machines and none of them having bookshelves. It made the bachelor smile again. This was a mismatch. Another sentence or two and she would lose interest in the kid and go back to her friends.

Now the bachelor was not an admirer of chubby women. He liked firm, athletic bodies and outdoor attitudes. He liked a walk in the woods with a backpack full of wine, cheese, and bread. This was a woman who took her hikes on the couch with a bagful of chocolate chip cookies. Still, he was smiling, enjoying her talk, and it had been a while since he had smiled at the mere pleasure of a woman's conversation.

Looking around, he found a small wooden bowl of thirst-inducing peanuts; the Trojan ponies of the bar world. He reached around the flautist and introduced himself, offering her the bowl.

"My caviar," he said, "is all at home. May I offer you some of these for the time being?"

She laughed. He suggested that the bar was getting crowded and perhaps the three of them should move to a table, enjoy the music more, and all that. . . .

The boy hung back, mumbled something about his flute, and disappeared. At the table, they traded jokes, the woman skewering two of his favorite prejudices within as many minutes. For a few seconds, they watched a woman at the bar play with an outrageous string of pearls. "I wonder if she's given them all names?" the woman asked.

"What would you name pearls?" the bachelor asked. "Fritz and Minnie?"

"Yeah—or Harbor and Bailey."

It was stupid repartee, more like an exchange of credentials than real talk, but it worked. They swapped opinions.

Est, California wine, and the Great Outdoors; he was in favor, she against. Small dogs, junk food, and television; vice versa.

They compared bona fides: She went to graduate school in pursuit of knowledge; he went to prolong his adolescence. He was city; she was suburbs. He was stick shift; she was automatic.

But mostly they laughed. He was good at making women laugh—it had been the core of his seduction technique for years. She was good at making him laugh, too, and that was for him a brand-new experience.

The band was starting its first number. A

man came up to their table, asked her to dance. She waved him away. She was talking about how absolutely unhousebroken her parents' aged Yorkshire terrier was. He was thinking that the dog and the cat would never get along and how this could put a limit on what might become of this conversation. Relieved, he dove back into talking.

They were cupping their ears against the music, reading lips in the din. It was dance or move. He asked her to dance. The bachelor was an enthusiastic dancer, graceful and uninhibited. The woman was wild, a round little snake in heat.

She drove him home after the bar closed but didn't go in. She was not a first-date sort of woman. So they sat in her car and talked and necked and pawed until his fatigue convinced his lust that it was time to say good night. He took her phone number and made a date for dinner the next evening.

The bachelor woke up con- fused. He had the absurd and uninvited vision that if he pursued this woman, he would end up marrying her. He would marry her because in her he finally had someone his own age to play with. She was complicated and interesting and funny. It was a little bit like being with the cat. When they talked, she was completely there, not scanning the room for someone richer or better. Or maybe he'd marry her for that lusty promise he saw in her eyes. She seemed like a woman who kept her promises.

But she was too heavy—maybe weighed more than he did—not the sort of woman he wanted at all. Still there was something about her, some carnal sparkle in her eyes and in her talk. . . .

He knew that this was a woman who wouldn't . . . no, couldn't, play the girl-friend's game. She was smart, he thought, maybe even smart enough to know that she didn't have to scheme every minute.

Not bad. Not good, not good at all.

The crazy vision of mar-
riage to a fat, funny woman gave way to a
pang of longing for the girlfriend. He
reminded himself that with any other
woman, he'd always miss the girlfriend, but
the truth was that he'd miss the high drama
of her. And he'd miss the women in
between just as much.

The bachelor stewed the day away, sim-
mering himself in various juices. He put the
card with the woman's phone number on
his dresser, looked at it half a dozen times,
and didn't call her. He went out that night

with a few of his friends, turning up after a long absence in places that he used to visit with the girlfriend. He left his answering machine off.

A few days later, he called
her. He wouldn't have been able to say why
he did any more than he could have said
why he hadn't when he was supposed to.

The woman was cool, unimpressed with a
guy who stood her up, not invested enough
in the situation to be angry. He was scrambling, not knowing why, trying to make it up
to her. He tried Charm, then Wit. When he
got to Self-Abasement, she wavered. At
Extravagant Promises, she gave in and agreed
to see him the next night.

The bachelor hung up the phone and sank into confused immobility. At a more self-reflective moment, he might have grasped the truth. The fact was that he had become comfortable with his romantic life: on-again, off-again with the girlfriend and plenty of room in between for wild times with attractive strangers. Some people might have compared his romantic routine to watching sports on television. It gave him drama, passion, variety, and not much responsibility.

This woman looked like a threat to all that.

What jolted him out of his stupor was the thrill of a project: a seduction dinner! He was excited, too, by the chance to talk to her again. It had been a long time, he realized, since he had been with someone whose talk was a thrill in itself.

The day was rainy and the night came cool. It was an evening better suited for old loves than new flames. He wondered if she would stand him up. She was twenty minutes late, breezing in with a bouquet of tulips and a handshake.

She sat on a stool in his kitchen while he fiddled with risotto and apologies. She directed his attention back to risotto and then to a story about a bachelor she once knew who was so in love with his own cooking that he was likely to be eating it alone for a long time. Properly cautioned on moderation, he kept stirring, letting the homey scent of broth and the sexy smell of herbs do their work.

A half hour later, they finished eating the creamy rice, and the woman was pushing a mushroom around the plate with her fork. The cat, who still hid at the approach of strangers, strolled out from beneath the couch and jumped onto the woman's lap.

"Hiya, handsome," the woman said. "What's his name?"

"It's Frankie, and she's a girl."

"Hello, Frankie," the woman said as her fingers found a magic spot between the cat's ears. "You're very pretty."

She scratched the spot and the cat pushed against her scratching, eyes closed, purr volume up. She murmured some things to the cat that he couldn't quite catch, then turned her attention back to him. Other women talked to him about the cat, using the cat as a way to relate to him. This woman talked to the cat.

"I'd help you clear the dishes, but as you can see, I've got a cat on my lap."

Back in the kitchen, he busied himself with plates. His seafood manicotti were bubbling in their sauce. It took two minutes to steam the long, skinny green beans, fuss with arrangements, dribble vinegar and herb butter, open the wine. He wondered how his seduction strategy was going.

He picked a pinot noir, scarlet and light-bodied, hoping to provoke a red wine with fish comment. She ignored his choice, took a polite sip, and asked for a glass of water.

Dessert was a chocolate crepe with fresh raspberry filling and a trickle of vanilla sauce. She ate hers without saying a word, modestly accepted a second helping, and ate that, too.

He cleared the dessert dishes and suggested they retire to the living room for a cordial. As he walked her to the couch, he called, "Frankie . . . C'mon, sweetie . . ." and by the time they sat down, the cat was there, nuzzling his hand. The woman was impressed.

"How did you train her to do that?" she asked.

"I just made sure that whenever she heard her name, something good was happening. After a while, I guess she just put it together. She hears her name and knows that something good is happening. Wouldn't you want to hang around if you knew you were going to be fed and petted?"

"I guess I would . . . but you know that probably works better with animals than it does with people."

"What do you mean?"

"Haven't you ever noticed that some people seem to hang around places where bad stuff happens? You know, where they get put down and rejected?"

The bachelor felt her looking at him. He looked back. It was possible, of course, that she'd been reading his mail or interviewing a few of his friends and knew all about his life with the girlfriend. Possible but not likely.

Still, there was something in her look. He gulped like a goldfish for a minute, trying to suck an idea off the surface of his pond—something clever in defense of "some people"—anything clever at all. And then he gave up. He didn't want to joust with this woman.

"I think I've been one of those people myself," he said, putting on a wise, self-mocking smile, hoping to get a few points for sincerity.

She didn't reply or even smile back. Instead, she looked at him and her eyes flickered a little downward squeeze of sadness.

"I guess it's a good thing we have cats to show us the right way sometimes."

They drank and talked and smoked cigarettes. They discussed her work, his past, their current mutual sense of being at a crossroads, their confusions about what each might do next. They laughed a lot. She was funny and not very critical. He let himself be silly in a way that he hadn't been in a long time. They listened to Bach; they listened to Gershwin. They danced to the Gershwin, then tried dancing to the Bach. They laughed some more and the bachelor was surprised to feel so much at home in his own house.

The next morning they
drank coffee and pretended that they each
had something to do that was more important than spending the day with each other.
He showed her the game that he and the cat
played with the fishing pole. She tried the
person's part, then she tried the cat's. She
christened the game Catfishing, and they
spent a giggly half hour playing it. They had
a third cup of coffee on the couch. She took
clumsy leave; he said an awkward good-bye.

The bachelor walked her to her car and
returned, confused, to the house. He was

delighted with this wise and funny woman, already half in love with her. He was appalled that he felt this way about someone with a body like hers. The lust of novelty was bound to wear off quickly and then what would he do? He noticed the cat, curled up in the indentation on the couch that the woman had just left.

A month later, the woman was taking her phone calls at his house and rearranging the furniture one piece at a time. The bachelor discovered that the woman had other charms besides her wit.

She was unrelenting in her goodness. His worst moods didn't make a dent in it. Somehow she knew that if he was grouchy or withdrawn it meant that he was suffering. She took his best as a personal gift to her and saw his worst as a piece of odd, misdirected mail. She quickly became the sunlight in which a long-frozen part of him melted.

She was also blessed, as he had suspected when they met, with an overwhelming sensuality. Her lovemaking left him exhausted, happy, and puzzled. She was not at all like the athletic beauties for whom he lusted. She didn't touch some magic switch and turn him on like the girlfriend. And still. And still there was something so deeply satisfying about holding her and loving her that he felt like he'd discovered a different dimension to love.

The best part was that he was a better man with her around—wittier, kinder, happier. The anxious lock on his heart had come undone.

They wasted time together.
One day they walked along antique row
with a million mythical dollars to spend. By
the second store, they were spending it all
on each other. He bought her a big lizard
brooch paved with rhinestones, braces of
crystal perfume bottles, and huge dangly
pink coral earrings. She traded the earrings
in for a deco plastic bracelet. She bought
him a Mazda, a giant brass telescope, and a
daguerreotype of a woman dressed in feath-
ers. Their imaginary million was barely
touched, so they bought a vanity that was

inlaid with ivory, a voluptuously carved sleigh bed, and a rococo tilting mirror. They joked about where they might place the mirror.

Before they left, they used some real money. He bought her a tiny pin with a picture of Elvis on it. She bought him a postcard of a couple negotiating a bay at the Jersey shore in a rowboat with a wineglass transom.

That night as he cooked dinner, the girlfriend called. She was thinking about him, wanted to hear his voice. She said this wistfully, as if they had been separated by grand forces—the Berlin Wall or the Montague-Capulet feud. He was brushed by the eroticism of hearing her voice, but in a distant, impersonal way, as if she were a sexy billboard glimpsed from a train.

He made deliberate cooking sounds while they spoke. He said good night, citing exacting dinner preparations, hoping she would draw conclusions. He congratulated himself, even mistook the tingle of his tiny triumph for a sign of being done with her.

The woman may have overheard something else in his voice. She asked with a raised eyebrow; he denied with a change of subject. No sense making her feel insecure, he thought.

One evening at sunset, the bachelor opened the windows again to let fresh-air smells in the house. He pointedly left the large front window closed. The cat, a leggy adolescent now, jumped over the cold radiator and onto the windowsill that faced the street. The bachelor took pictures of her silhouetted against the yellow brick buildings across the street.

He went outside to take a few more shots of her before the light died. And then he stood on the sidewalk admiring her, the gray of her coat only a shade or two lighter than the darkness of the house.

He was feeling pretty fortunate when he heard a voice call his name from halfway down the block. It was an old friend, someone he knew from a few towns ago, heading up the street, carrying a six-pack of beer.

"I thought I'd drop by and see how the hell you're doing . . . find out about the Great Romance." They walked up the steps together and found the cat sitting, as composed as an Egyptian ornament, just inside the door.

The bachelor put down his camera and scooped up the cat. He was grinning. She didn't run. The opening door now meant him.

He brought the woman to other people's exhibits even though her enthusiasm was well muted. One night, at the opening of a show that consisted of giant silk-screened numbers, he left her in the crowd and went off to talk with a dealer. When he was done with the dealer, he waved to her briefly and headed off to engage two willowy models who showed up at these things. He was a few sentences into the models when he felt the woman at his side. She touched his arm, introduced herself to the ladies, and a few words later steered him off to the side, away from the crowd, and next to a giant black 6 on a yellow field.

"Why did you take off like that?" she said.

"Take off like what?"

Her face composed itself into the concentrated mask of a person about to explain herself in a foreign language. "When we walked in the door, you practically pushed me away from you and trotted off to talk to someone else."

"Yes . . . yes . . . I guess I did." He looked embarrassed.

"Well, what's up? Was it something I said about resemblances of certain art works to things I'd recently seen in supermarket windows? Or are you a little bit shy about introducing me to your friends?"

Art always made the bachelor honest. He had heard the story of a man who loved a homely woman, who was embarrassed to be seen with her in public. The fellow in the story handled the problem by faking a fear of crowds. The bachelor had always thought that the guy was a worm. He examined himself for signs. A careful minute passed.

"No. I guess it's . . ." And then he started to laugh.

"What?"

"Well, didn't you want me to? I mean, wouldn't you prefer that I go off and let you mingle? I mean . . . I didn't want to crowd you."

"Actually, that was not what I had in mind. I came here with you so I could be with you. At least I thought I did. Maybe I came here to see exactly what colors single digits are wearing this year." She was smiling by now; he was still squirming.

So he told her about the girlfriend, about how she always insisted on being left alone at parties, how she didn't want to seem "joined at the hip."

"Listen, I'm not that girlfriend. She sounds like she was always looking around for somebody better. I'll bet that every once in a while she found someone, too."

"Yeah, as a matter of fact, sometimes she did."

"I'll bet she even made you think that it was your fault when she did."

They were facing each other, so close that they could talk below the noise of the crowd. She put her drink on the floor and squeezed his arms just above the elbows.

"She didn't want to be with you and I do. Are you sure you want to be with me?"

The bachelor took some time to answer and the woman held on. She liked him, wanted to be with him . . . *wanted* . . . and yes, he had enjoyed the chances to flirt, which the girlfriend had given him, but this woman, this woman wanted to be with him . . . she liked him. It might not be the easiest trade, but it could be a good one.

"Let's go someplace quieter," he said, hugging her quickly. He pulled in his breath to keep unseemly feelings from popping out, unsure about just what emotion he was holding in.

Out on the street they walked arm in arm, silently, listening to the noise of the gallery fade behind them.

At the first corner the woman said, "I really liked that 6, but of course we can't afford it. Maybe we could buy something smaller, like, oh, let's say a 3?"

The next day, the cat was watching him fold and sort a pile of laundry that he had just brought back from the Laundromat. She seemed fascinated by the way a pair of socks, folded and tucked into a ball, would roll when he tossed them into a pile on the edge of his bed. This was a thing to be investigated, smelled, batted, pounced on.

The bachelor, always eager to be distracted from laundry, turned up the volume. He pulled a ball of clean white sweat socks away from her in short, jerky starts. She arched her back, jumped to the side, figured angles, gauged distances. She feinted with her left paw, pulled back, sprang to the other side. She struck with a right, claws extended, digging into the fabric and rolling on her back, the white cotton knit prey a doomed and helpless victim.

He laughed in the way we do at the ferocity of the tiny, but he was impressed, too. Whatever this little dance was or meant, she was very good at it—an athlete, a furry little shortstop who wasn't going to let much get by her.

He let go of the socks, then she, no longer interested in them now that they were truly dead, let go, too, and looked at him. Her face was, he would have sworn, a mask of immobile inquisition. So? What? Now?

The bachelor was not a stupid man, so he got the idea fairly quickly. Pinching a single layer of the socks between his thumb and forefinger, he bounced them wildly from side to side, around her, behind her. She cowered. What was this? The evil grandfather of the thing she just killed? She flipped to her back, claws ready: it would be a fight to the death. The thing dropped on her. It was almost as big as she was, but she rolled to the side and threw it off her. She kept rolling until she was standing up, then she jumped back. She looked at him. He was still there, smiling. She attacked the socks, rolling and beating and clawing them halfway across the bed and then onto the floor.

She celebrated her victory with a sudden stop, a quiet paw lick—a poster kitten for the Nonchalance Foundation.

The bachelor was unsatisfied. He bent, scooped up the socks, and flipped them back on the bed. This time she lunged, grabbed them, and quickly let them go. She went back to grooming what must have been a very neglected paw.

Reminded of the rule Moving Socks Good, Still Socks Boring, he went back to his assignment. Socks fled, cat followed, cat always won.

He was amazed at her attention span. She was just as alert for the fifteenth round as she was for the first. What called his attention to her attention was the flagging of his own attention. Tired of the game, he threw the socks to the side, petted her, and went back to making clothes piles.

Two folded T-shirts and a pair of jeans later, the kitten had struggled to the middle of his laundry pile, dragging the socks with her. She picked her spot, stopped, let go of the socks, pushed them toward him with a paw, sat, and looked up.

He let himself be trained and in a little while they both had learned to play Fetch.

She dragged the socks to him, they played;
he threw them away, she fetched them back.
A half hour later, the kitten fell asleep and
the bachelor felt unaccountably happy and
proud of himself.

A few days later, the woman came home from grocery shopping with a small bag of goodies and a large white tube under her arm. The tube, unrolled, contained the paper signs that had advertised last week's specials. There was a deco 4 romancing a Rubenesque 9, two buxom 5s in a line, and more. They settled on the yin and yang of "Bananas 3 lb. 69¢" and taped it on the wall above the fireplace. They crumpled up the rest of the signs and put them in the fireplace, where he kept the junk mail.

He turned the food in the grocery bag

into a snack, and they ate together on the couch, enjoying their new art and warming themselves by the flames of last week's sales. They talked about what they might do with the thousands of dollars they saved by not buying an original print at the gallery.

The bachelor thought of his house as a cave with windows—shelter for him and his work and, now, the cat. There was no entry closet in the old row-house, so the couch and the banister became coatracks. In times of wifty spring weather, five or six coats could pile up just inside the front door. The woman added her own two or three and the coats became a nation, roommates in their own right.

The woman never objected, although she was hardly a coat-on-the-couch sort of person. Then, the day after she added to his art collection, she added something else: a spindly, bentwood, ball-bearing-spinning coat-rack, alien arms reaching for the ceiling.

She dragged it through the front door and presented it to him. She was so excited about its arrival that he only blinked once or twice as he collected and stacked their coats on it.

It bothered him for a moment, this prissy polished thing right inside his front door. But she seemed pleased with herself, so he gave the coatrack a spin and her a kiss.

Some days give you kittens, he thought, and some days give you coatracks.

Later that day, the phone rang while he was deep in his work.

"Would you get that?" he said, smiling at himself. Sure, answer my phone, furnish my house.

The ringing stopped, and a few seconds later the woman stuck her head through the door of his studio.

"If a woman answers," she said, counting on him to translate from the joke to the hangup. She looked at him for a long moment with eyes that said, "Wanna tell me about it?"

He didn't, couldn't, and that made him cranky. The cold shadow of the girlfriend fell on their day.

The bachelor and the woman were sitting on the front steps of his house, enjoying the rare cool breeze of a summer night. He held a glass of white wine; she had some freshly made lemonade. The front door was open behind them to help the wind sweep the sweat of a Philadelphia summer from the house.

Quietly, they talked a little as one star appeared, then ten, then a tribe of them, bright enough to push their way past the streetlights. Occasionally the bachelor and the woman waved to one of the neighbors, who had by now grown as used to seeing her as him. But mostly they were quiet, and then they fell silent, enjoying the night and each other.

The silence was shaken apart by a low, rumbling purr. The cat, who had shied back from the sound of the opening door, was standing beside the woman, rubbing against her, demanding.

"She hasn't been outside since I found her!" the bachelor said.

"She probably couldn't get out past all those coats," the woman said, lifting the cat to her lap. The cat looked at him, blinked, and settled in to be stroked as if she always hung around outside, caressed to the sound of the passing traffic.

The next morning, he brought the woman coffee in bed. The cat followed him down the stairs to the kitchen and up the stairs again to the bedroom. She posted herself on the windowsill and studied the street while they sipped and adjusted themselves to the grim inevitability of waking up.

"Here," the bachelor said to the woman, "I'm going to start your day with a cat lesson. Are you ready?"

"As long as it doesn't require anything hard, like being fully conscious or licking my own fur."

"No, nothing so difficult as that. I'm going to show you how to lure a cat."

"I didn't think they were lurable."

"They are, and if you're willing to swear to use your new-found powers only for good, the lesson can begin."

"Consider it sworn."

He set his coffee cup down and began to make a series of squeaky lip noises, sounds that would have most people reaching for the oil can. The cat swiveled her head toward them without moving an unnecessary muscle.

The woman began a narration in a voice made up of equal parts Disney nature movie and *Twilight Zone*.

"His quarry responds to the call with the economy of movement characteristic of her species."

The bachelor grabbed a few fingers' worth of bedclothes and wiggled them.

"Frankie . . . Frankie . . . Frankie . . ."

"Having aroused her curiosity, the cat trapper goes to the second stage of his plan."

The cat turned, pivoting on her hind legs on the narrow sill and dropping to the low sideboard below. Two small, light-footed jumps and she was on the bed. All four paws landed in a tight circle at the very corner farthest from him.

"Her curiosity overcoming her caution, the cat advances farther into the trap."

The bachelor said her name again, tickling the covers slowly and more sensuously than before. The cat advanced with a tiny leap over the woman's legs to a spot just out of the bachelor's reach.

"The wily trapper seizes his opportunity and springs on the unsuspecting . . ."

"Oh, no, that would be the wrong way," said the bachelor. "He does something much more clever than that. Behold the right way."

As the cat took a tentative step toward him, the bachelor turned away. He lay back on his side, his hand making one circuit of his hip and then stopping.

"The clever cat hunter . . . ignores his quarry?"

"No, no, O foolish one, I'm letting her know that I don't need her to come to me, that it's not desperate or urgent or anything . . . just that this is where the love and the petting are."

No sooner had he explained than the cat appeared on the top of his hip, purring, nuzzling, and demanding his attention. "And that, my dear, is the right way to lure a cat."

"Amazing!" the woman said. "I think that's amazing. How long did it take you to teach her that?"

"I didn't teach it to her at all."

"No?"

"No, she taught it to me."

One morning, when they woke up together with the cat between them, he said to the woman, "Did you ever notice that when you smile at her, she starts purring?"

"I noticed," the woman said, "that whenever she purrs at you, you start smiling."

Later that day, the woman told him over lunch that it was time for her to stop taking up space in the guest room of her friend's place. She wanted to move in with him. She said it casually, like a thing assumed, and he had been thinking about it himself. But her request chilled him.

Could they just sort of, umm . . . see each other? He needed more time, you see, more time to . . . umm . . . well, more time. He didn't say what he wanted was a chance to date more of those gazelle-bodied beauties. He didn't say he imagined himself to be a reckless adventurer, a tough guy with women and she would spoil that image forever.

It didn't matter that he was in fact no tough guy but a man who treasured women. For the moment, he ached for a time to be tough. He didn't know that the longing to be free wasn't really a part of him, that it was more a tribute of imitation to the girlfriend who left him. He didn't even know that the desire to please a lover can sometimes outlive the love itself.

In fairness to him, he may not have known what he needed the time for. As he looked across the table at her, he was panicked, not calculating.

The woman started to cry—no sobs or shakes—her eyes filling up slowly. He reached for her, but she brushed his hand away. No weepy victories for her.

"I'm sorry, I really am," the bachelor said. "It's just that everything has gone so fast. I need a chance to think about all this. Why can't I have that?"

The woman, who had often noticed the general incompetence of men, had a sudden vision of its source. Whatever this man thought, he actually felt that completing something, making himself whole, would be a loss. The knowledge didn't make her happy, but she would remember it nonetheless.

They talked for another hour. She tried to lead him to a vision of his future, to invoke the happiness that he so evidently felt in her presence. She asked him for coffee and watched the pleasure he took in making it for her. His heart warmed in the making of it, but he fell back to his moronic mantra, "I need more time."

She had done all she could. Any more talking would spoil something for her. She knew she could make it easy for herself and spin this conversation until she felt disgust instead of frustrated love. She could leave with relief instead of sadness.

Instead, she stood up and said, "I would love to give you more time. I would give you that if I had it to give . . . of course I would." Her voice had the slow cadence of a person who is discovering the truth of what she says as she's saying it. "I love you so much, but I don't have time to give you. If you don't want me here, I will go away, but I couldn't be half in your life and half out. I'll give you some time to decide.

"There's a friend I've been wanting to visit. I'll be back on Saturday, that's four days from now. Let's say noon. I'll make it easy for you: If you're here, I'll take that to mean you want me to stay. If you're not . . . well, I'll say good-bye to the cat, get my things, and go. And I'll be very sad for you." She reached down and touched his cheek as she said the words "sad for you," and he felt a bubble of sadness rising up in him.

She sat for a minute, looking toward the front of the house, toward the door. The bachelor was hit—wham, bam. His panic, her pain. For a second he looked at the chubby flesh on her upper arm. Looking at her dulled his sensitivity to her, and he hated himself for being so easily blinded.

A few minutes later she had packed her things and was gone.

That night he stayed home until almost midnight. He worked on some pictures that had no commercial value and tried not to think about the woman.

After dinner, he got out the fishing pole and snuck up on all fours on the sleeping cat. From behind the sofa, he brushed her gently with the lure. She grabbed it with extended claws almost before her eyes opened. He pulled it away and she rolled to her feet, following it along the rug, turning surely to snag it just as it reached the slippery wood floor.

She rolled on her back, all four claws tearing at her victim. The bachelor let the line go slack. In a few seconds, the cat, apparently shocked by the sudden death of the prey, stopped. On her feet again, her eyes met his. She batted the lure away with (Was it possible?) a touch of irritation and walked directly to him. He sat on the floor holding her on his lap and listening to the house for what seemed like a long time.

Around midnight, he went out to his neighborhood bar, just to clear the brain and have a friendly drink. If he'd been able to be honest, he would have admitted that he wondered if the woman would be there, or if some other woman might show up and help him not think about what he was going to do.

The woman wasn't there. She was gone and he felt the presence of her absence; he had a drink and went home. She wasn't there either, although he had stupidly expected that she might be. It was a long time before he went to sleep, and he found himself wishing that he could call her. It wasn't that he had anything to say, no decision to announce: He just wanted to hear her voice, to break the spell of her being gone.

*He woke up the next morn-*ing numb and unrested. He swung his feet out of bed and found himself staring at his small collection of framed personal photographs. They stood on a walnut slab raised on blocks that served as the sideboard to his bed, which was itself nothing more than a mattress and box spring on a heavily carpeted floor. There were two pictures of his parents, one of his favorite uncle in riding costume, and another of a boy aged twelve or so. The boy, full-length against a chain-link fence, is throwing a ball in a gentle juggling fashion in the air. The camera's shutter has stretched the roundness of the ball along its height, and the boy's eyes seem to be looking ahead along its path—at a point some six or eight inches above the ball.

The bachelor had used his first camera to take that picture when he was eleven years old. It was the image of his best friend: a boy named David. David had died a child's death from a child's disease a few months after the picture was taken. The bachelor had forgotten the name of the sickness that killed him. He had come to think of the sickness as a dart thrown from somewhere that struck David because it had to strike somebody.

David had been the farsighted one, the leader of their little group, general of boyhood forts and captain of pick-up teams. David had not stayed forever young in the bachelor's mind in the way that those who

die in childhood are supposed to. He had
instead aged along with the bachelor. He
had become a contemporary, an oracle, even
the custodian of the bachelor's secret belief
that photographs had the power of life and
death.

But David and David's picture had no
advice for him, and he went downstairs
emptier than when he had woken up.

The phone rang while he was having coffee and cat. It was the girl-friend.

"Hi, I've been thinking about you."

"Really?" the bachelor said, aroused by the sound of her voice and wary at the same time.

"Really. Intensely, as a matter of fact. What have you been up to?"

"Lots of interesting things . . . been really busy."

"Yeah? Me, too . . . umm . . . I was wondering if you had time for a drink this afternoon?" He thought quickly about how the woman would see him having a drink with his old girlfriend. She would see it as an indication of his choice.

She would be wrong, of course. Meeting the girlfriend was a test, a purely diagnostic drink, just a dip of the old litmus paper to see how blue it could get. So he named a time later that day and she named a cute little place on the other side of town.

He arrived at the bar a few minutes late just to show her . . . something. She wasn't there and he thought about leaving. Instead, he ordered a drink and sat at the bar underneath a giant fern. The girlfriend came in when he had just about finished. She was breathless, smiling, and carrying a gym bag. She was wearing tiny shorts, the world's thinnest T-shirt, and ropy platform sandals. Her tan had been well maintained and there was a pair of Lolita-red heart-shaped sunglasses perched on top of her head. Child-like and sexy: It was pure, vintage girlfriend, just like the old days. Even the two women sitting at a corner table turned to look at her, and the room's erotic dimmer switch was turned up a notch.

She dragged a stool to within knee-touching distance, ignoring his glance at the clock. She ordered a vodka on the rocks with a cherry and a straw.

"How have you been?" Her smile was impossibly bright and the bachelor found himself buzzing with that hot energy she used to bring out in him.

She asked him about his work and about mutual friends. She didn't say anything about herself, didn't ask about the cat. There was much touching of arms and brushing of legs. Her cheeks hollowed as she sucked her way to the bottom of her glass. In a few minutes, as his drink neared empty, she picked up her bag and said, "Can you take a little walk with me? There's something I'd like you to see."

They walked half a block to a corner apartment building, a three-story turn-of-the-century model. A minute later he was standing in her new sun-splashed apartment. She put down her bag and walked over to the floor-to-ceiling window.

"What do you think?" she said, turning sideways and letting the sunlight undress her.

"I think it's just about perfect."

"I want to ask your opinion," she said, leading him away from the window and down a short hall to one of two bedrooms. The room was empty except for a few cardboard boxes, a drawing table, and a lamp.

"Do you think this would make a good studio for an artist?" she said, walking to the far corner of the room and bending down with her back to him to pick up some stray item from the floor. She straightened and looked back over her shoulder, caught him looking at her, and giggled. She turned and took a step in his direction.

She prompted him again. "What do you think?"

The bachelor had seen this movie before. They were at the part where she gives him the wonderful straight line, he gets a chance to be fabulously witty, and she pretends it was his masterly control of the situation that leads them to collapse together in a flurry of arms and legs. He felt static sparks, thought they might have been in his brain. He was considering responses, weighing his chances, as seduced by the skill of her offering as he was by her.

He smiled brightly. She smiled back and took her sunglasses off her head. She bit one bow and her eyes widened, a smile melting from around the white teeth. For a second he saw the cat and his smile became less electric, more gentle.

He took a step toward her without speaking. She leaned forward. There was a space, maybe a body's length between them. Her eyes were turning hard, impatient. Her look reminded him of something; he felt an anxious wave sweep over him and noticed that he had almost stopped breathing. He had to leave.

He looked down at his watch. "I really have to go . . . only had time for just a drink. I'll call you."

He felt himself cool down
as he left her air-conditioned apartment and
hit the hot street. He didn't understand the
feeling, but it made him happy.

As he walked, squinting in the afternoon
sun, he tried to remember the sick, anxious,
near-death feeling at the bottom of the girlfriend's rollercoaster. But there was something
buoyant about the moment and he failed.
He failed, too, when he tried to remember
the silver clear ringing of the woman's presence and the warmth she brought to his life.
He tried hard not to think about either feeling, and with that he was at last successful.

There was a message from the girlfriend waiting for him when he got home: . . . sorry he had to leave so soon . . . perhaps he could come to dinner, stay a bit longer . . . would he call so he could pick a time?

That night he called his two fishing buddies. They came by his house and he told them the story. They sat at his dining-room table with bottles of beer while the cat watched them from a cool radiator.

"What are you going to do?" one of the buddies asked.

"I don't know."

And that being a man's way of asking for advice, his friends fell to giving it.

"Look, you'll never know which one loves you more, so the question has to be

119

which woman lets you love *her* more," said the divorced one.

"Yeah, it's not how you feel about them—that's like trying to take your own temperature all the time. You gotta go with the one who makes you feel best about yourself," said the one who was between girlfriends.

The next day, the bach-
elor canceled his morning appointments
and grumped his way back to bed with extra
pillows and coffee. The cat joined him. She
seemed to be telling him something that he
couldn't quite translate. He saw whirling
images of the woman and the girlfriend.
The woman would be back tomorrow; he
expected her by noon.

He rolled the cat gently on her side and
stroked the fur of her belly. Heaven, he
thought, would have to be a place lined
with cat bellies.

The cat stroked him, too, rubbing her head into his chest. The best thing about the cat, he thought, is that the more you love her, the more she loves you back. He found himself singing to her:

> *Why can't a woman*
> *Be more like a cat?*

Then he noticed, as he petted her, how much a part her grace and physical beauty played in her appeal. How much like the girlfriend the cat was, how unlike the woman.

When the phone rang, and he heard the girlfriend's voice, he thought it was destiny itself calling. Of course they were meant to be together. Passion like theirs didn't exist for no reason.

"How about brunch tomorrow? Around eleven? I have a big surprise for you." Her voice oversweet, treacly, a spider-to-a-fly voice. Any conscious person would have been alerted, shocked into caution by it.

Tomorrow was Saturday, the day the woman would return—around noon, lunch time, brunch time, but he was only half aware of that awkward coincidence. He thought for a minute of his friends' advice. It sat lightly with him: Good wisdom for somebody else, but obviously beside his point, he said, as he always did to that voice. Yes, yes, of course. The girlfriend may have overacted her part, but she surely knew her audience.

And so the date was made and the bachelor settled into a cottony fog. The thing was done. He was going to brunch with his old girlfriend tomorrow, and so he guessed that he wouldn't . . . wouldn't have to think about it anymore.

*But he couldn't stop think-*ing about the woman any more than you could stop thinking about the fireplace when you were about to step out into the cold. So he busied himself.

He mopped floors, cleaned windows, and fixed a leaking sink drain. He bought lumber for a window box he'd been mean-ing to build and left it in a heap while he made sketches for a series of prints he'd dreamed up while toting the lumber home.

He forgot to eat. He made five enthusias-tic phone calls to art directors. The phone felt so natural that he used it to order some wood-carving tools, which he couldn't really afford. He always wanted to do some sculpture.

By nightfall, he had tuned himself into a very taut piano string. He drank most of a bottle of wine with his dinner and then called a few friends. Nobody wanted to talk as much as he did. He dusted off an old bar-bell and lifted it a few times, stopping to jot down a note about this great way to store drawings that occurred to him around the fifth curl.

At ten o'clock, he put on sneakers and went out jogging. By ten-thirty, he was standing in his neighborhood bar, drinking a Manhattan and wondering why everybody seemed so subdued. At eleven, he was home finishing his wine and lecturing the cat about the importance of keeping a positive outlook on life.

He slept the next morning until nine and woke up annoyed. Not enough sleep, too much time before his date. His percolating enthusiasm of the day before had left him; he was flat, prickly, and irritated.

As he left the house he remembered to leave the door open in case the woman had forgotten her key. She was always forgetting her key, he thought, feeling a stupid burst of love for her even as he was leaving her. She would find this empty house and she would understand, although he was glad he didn't have to explain it to her. He even wondered for a second if she could explain it to him.

And then he shook that thought off, flicked the door closed behind him, and conjured an image of the girlfriend. He crossed the street so far ahead of the black convertible that was cruising slowly down the block that he was surprised when he heard the horn and turned to see the car thrust forward in a sudden stop.

The rest he took in at once. The cat's scream full of horror and pain, his open front door across the street, the cursing of the driver. Four steps and he saw her, small and gray, the right rear side of her body beneath the tire, the puddle of her blood being squeezed on the blacktop.

By the time he reached the
vet's office, the stream of the cat's blood had
soaked his shirt front and was staining the
top of his pants. From a distance, it would
have seemed that the wounds were his. He
could feel her heartbeat growing fainter as
they blew past two waiting dogs and into the
surgery. The sharp barking of the two city
dogs, aroused as much by his fear as by the
cat's blood, rang in his ears as he placed the
cat on the table.

She lay on the steel table, her body very
still. From time to time, she would open her

eyes and faintly nuzzle his hand. The vet held back for a second, shaking her head. She was a doctor who clearly preferred her patients to their owners, but now she spared the bachelor a head bob of sympathy. She reached for a tray of instruments and bellowed for her assistant. There was more blood. How much blood could be in that little body?

The assistant pushed him back out into the waiting room. His protest only made the vet freeze, so he left. He did not want to let his cat die alone. In the waiting room, he felt the heat of the blood on his chest and looked without feeling at the horrified dog owners.

The assistant came out. "Doctor will do her best," she said in a voice that had no hope in it. She peeled off her paper smock and threw it away. The dogs' eyes followed its arc to the trash can. "She must really love you. I never saw a cat do that before . . . you know, nuzzle someone when they're hurt. Usually they scratch or bite."

Really loved him. His cat, his friend, the little creature who taught him to love, was bleeding to death from a crushed leg. He must have left the door a little bit open instead of merely unlocked. The cat, who had been so afraid of the outside, had squeezed her way through to follow him. He reached out a hand to steady himself and a moan came up from his chest.

He imagined her seeing the crack in the doorway. With closed eyes, he saw her cantering down the street to be with him. He heard himself breathing big greedy air gulps, his first real breaths in more than a day. He felt his numbness dissolve like ice breaking up on a springtime river. Then a rich and painful sense of aliveness swept over him. He felt the love and bravery of the cat's following him. He felt her pain and his own sense of loss.

He felt himself turning, returning. He looked down at his own hands. He closed his eyes, squeezing them hard against the light from the waiting-room window. When he opened them again, he thought he saw a vision of a face.

The clock in the waiting room stood at 12:05. He reached for the vet's telephone and dialed his own number.

Epilogue

The house was built on the slope of a grassy hill at the edge of a woods. An astonishing wall of glass faced the downhill side and in the wash of sunlight that came through the glass and the trees, a six-year-old girl was sitting on the floor holding a gray cat. The girl was rocking back and forth and murmuring baby talk to the cat. The cat, who had one crooked paw jutting grotesquely out of the little girl's embrace, was wearing the resigned look of the truly trapped.

"Daddy," the little girl said to the man

who was sitting on the couch nearby and sketching on a large spiral-bound pad, "isn't my kitty the cutest·kitty?"

When the man answered his voice didn't sound like the voice of a person who had been interrupted. He sounded almost as if he had been waiting all along, killing time with his sketchbook until she asked her question. "Yes, sweetie, she is."

The cat struggled, the little girl squeezed the cat some more, and the cat's eyes seemed to bulge from it.

"Hey," her daddy said, "you be careful with my cat. She's sixteen years old and she's not made of rubber. Put her down and do it the Right Way."

The little girl put the cat on the carpet and did what Daddy had carefully taught her. She lightly stroked the cat between the ears. The cat, freshly sprung, decided to make a break for it. The girl lunged, and her daddy said, "Uh-uh, baby, do it the Right Way: just love her, don't need her so much."

The little girl settled back and made whispering sounds to the cat, who took a few limping strides away from her and then stopped and sat. The man, sure that he had the best seat in town, wondered if he had a joy circuit breaker, something that would trip and protect him from bursting.

The girl whispered, the cat walked back and stopped next to her, one twisted foot still in the air as if to indicate just how tentative her return was. The girl reached out and used one index finger to scratch between the cat's ears. The man could see a dash of sunlight in the little girl's green eyes.

"Look, Daddy, I'm doing it the Right Way."

"Yes, you are, my love."

By the time the cat was settled in the little girl's lap, a cloud had blocked the sun and the shadows of the girl and the cat were smudged and then gone.

"Daddy, didn't you save her life once?"

"Yes, honey, and then she saved mine."

"Will you tell me the story of how Frankie saved your life?"

"Yes, honey, I will. I certainly will."

bachelor's cat *n* **1**: a person, pet, or preoccupation that enters a man's life and eases his transition to commitment; (by extension) a forerunner, something that points the way to a higher stage of development **2**: the nonhuman object of one's special attention and devotion

L. F. HOFFMAN is Lynn Hoffman, Ph.D., a food and wine critic in Philadelphia. He has also worked as a chef, bartender, and merchant seaman.